To Helena,

Happy Reading

MMcL

PAY DAY AND OTHER TEABREAK TALES

Michelle Mclean

For C and L.

With love.

Don't read this until you're older.

PAY DAY AND OTHER TEABREAK TALES

Contents

ACKNOWLEDGEMENTS

This collection of stories started out as a series of writing assignments for the Creative Writing element of my Bachelors Degree. I am grateful to my tutor Gill Ryland for her funny and forthright feedback throughout that course and for reigniting my love of writing.

My thanks also to Dympna McCarton who encouraged ten-year-old me to write and remains, several decades later, a huge source of encouragement. Her letters always contain news clippings about books and writers - the hints have not been lost on this lifelong pupil of hers.

I have the best cheerleading squad made up of my husband, family and friends. I am forever grateful for their support and belief in me.

PAY DAY

I stood on the doorstep, smiling and waving to the back of Malcolm's black Range Rover. I watched as it headed past the coiffured conifers and down towards the towering electric gates which slid open on his approach. He tooted twice, stuck a liver-spotted hand out of the window and then he was gone.

I immediately dropped my smile and stretched my aching jaw. Thomas, our gardener, was tending to a raised bed near the steps and he gave me a knowing look when he saw me gurning. I stepped back inside the house and quickly closed the door.

After putting on my jacket, I gave myself the once over in the ornate mirror in the hall. There was a huge vase of flowers on the glass table under it and I crinkled my nose at the overpowering smell of Longiflorum.

'Going out, Jessica?' said a sharp voice from further along the hallway. It was the housekeeper creeping up on me, like a noxious fart, as usual.

'Yes Sally,' I replied. 'Yoga class.'

'Yoga?' she asked. I caught her glance down at my ripped skinny jeans and high heeled boots. She

2

raised half of her monobrow.

'That's what I said.'

'Will you be going for lunch after your...yoga?'

'Nope. I'll be back in time to eat with Malcolm.'

'I'll have something ready for one thirty then.'

'One thirty will be fine,' We eyed each other for a moment and I felt a flicker of satisfaction when she looked away first. 'And please do something about these lilies whilst I'm out, Sally. They're so...funereal. We need Lisianthus, Bouvardia, Gerberas. You know, something more youthful.'

Sally's thin lips disappeared entirely, as she caged whatever words were threatening to escape her mouth. Lilies had been a favourite of Malcolm's first wife. I grabbed my bag and left, smirking. The nosey old bat could think what she liked, I was in charge now. Well almost. Malcolm had given me free reign over all of the domestic arrangements but one.

'She's part of the family, dear. Twenty-five years she's worked for me, almost longer than you've been alive!' and he'd laughed at his own stupid joke.

'She doesn't like me,' I'd whined. 'And she's weird.' It was all the explanation I could offer. I'd sound ridiculous if I confessed that I thought she was spying on me. I had a feeling he'd take her side anyway.

'She stays.' And that had been his final word on it.

So, Sally and I had spent the last six months participating in a petty power struggle. I'd move furniture around, she'd move it back. I bought new foods for Malcolm to try, she'd cook his favourites. Even my knicker draw wasn't off limits. I'd rummage through each morning and by the evening, I'd find the silky fabrics arranged back into neat little piles.

I wasn't worried though. Growing up, I had seen off plenty of overbearing and nosey women. Teachers, social workers, foster mums – they had all tried to interfere in my life. I could suffer Sally a while longer.

I climbed into my Mercedes and inhaled the divine, new car smell. I did this every morning, just sitting for a moment taking it all in before I turned the ignition on. My form of meditation.

This morning I had just enough time to call into the retail centre before heading out of town for a meeting. It was a short drive and I knew I wouldn't pass any of Malcolm's friends or rather, their wives.

Wednesday mornings were reserved for spin class followed by brunch at the Health Club and I wasn't invited.

I pulled into the retail centre car park, parking over the dividing line between two bays. It was cloudy but I put on my sunglasses anyway, slid my arm through the handles of my oversized handbag and went into the main department store.

I was conscious of my metal tips clacking loudly against the sparkling, tiled floor as I strode towards womenswear. It drew the attention of the salesgirls, eager to spray me with the latest perfumes or smudge the back of my hand with a new lipstick.

I quickly selected a bright yellow clutch with the designer's signature emblazoned across it in bold, red stitching. Feeling frivolous, I added the matching purse. Then, just before I left, I spotted a Swarovski phone charm, so I had that too then got on my way.

I felt upbeat and flicked the digital radio in my car over to Capital FM. Crapital, Malcolm called it. What did he know? I turned the volume up and sang along as I drove through light traffic to my meeting.

*

The shouts and laughter from a group of youths passing

my maisonette, ripped me out of my sleep. My eyes were being assaulted by the sun streaming in through my thin curtains and I buried my face under the duvet.

My brain had steel capped boots on and was trying to march out of my skull, whilst my tongue felt three sizes too big for my mouth. I stuck a bare arm out from under the duvet and felt around on my bedside cabinet for some paracetamol and whatever else I had. *Bingo.* I pulled myself up and washed down some tablets with the warm dregs from last night's vodka and Redbull.

'Shit!' I cursed, when I saw the time on my phone. I knew I should rush, try and be on time for once, but my mojo wouldn't kick in until the tablets did. I sat back against the spongy headboard and checked my Facebook, finally getting up when I had run out of scrolling to do.

On my way out, I poked my head around Jayden's door and saw that he had got himself off to school. His bed was made and his room was immaculate as usual, a sharp contrast to the rest of our gaff. Perhaps I could get the place sorted this afternoon, that would be a nice surprise for him. It might even encourage him to bring a mate round.

The bus ride was short but the pungent smell of weed wafting down from the top deck, coupled with my empty stomach, made me feel woozy. I held onto the seat in front and closed my eyes for a moment. Only it wasn't a moment.

'Oi driver! Let me out 'ere mate!' I called, holding my finger down on the bell as I stood up.

'Next stop is Old Fox Hill,' the driver said without looking at me.

'I can jump out right here,' I replied as we slowed for some traffic lights but he kept his head straight and didn't reply.

I slammed my hand against the emergency release button and the doors snapped open. 'Twat!' I yelled as I jumped out onto the pavement.

It was a bit of a walk back and as I puffed along the pavement, I scolded myself for the extra weight I was carrying. I was red-faced and damp under the arms when I arrived at The Fox.

The pub was half empty. Just a few regulars huddled near the bar having an early hair of the dog and a couple of lads playing pool, their school ties stuffed in their back pockets. Fat Sam was perched on a stool behind the bar, watching the horse racing. He looked up, saw me and nodded in the direction of the furthest corner.

She was there, at our usual table, with a glass of fizzy water. Despite the gloomy interior, she had on a ridiculously large pair of sunglasses. She looked polished and I pulled down my grubby top, conscious that my arse was almost visible in my ancient, stretched out leggings.

I flopped down into the seat opposite her and threw my backpack on the floor. She said nothing but took a deliberate, slow look at her flashy watch.

'Morning. You alright?' I asked. I folded my arms onto the table and it wobbled, nearly upsetting her drink.

'Yes fine. You? Jayden?' She held onto her glass with one hand and tried to adjust the table with the other.

'Same old, same old,' I shrugged.

She reached under the table, stuffing a beer mat under one of the legs and then took something from her massive handbag. She shoved it into my open backpack.

'The clutch bag is amazing and was quite tricky to acquire,' she said. 'The staff were very attentive and barely left me alone long enough to take it.' I nodded my

8

thanks.

I couldn't get used to this funny new accent of hers. She sounded strange with her 'rathers' and 'acquires' and I wanted to tease her. I thought better of it though, she had no sense of humour anymore.

We sat in silence for a few moments and she shifted around in her seat. She stared into her glass of water, twirling the straw with a slim manicured finger.

'So erm, how's things up at the big house?' I asked. 'Still ain't had an invite.'

'You know we don't have visitors,' she said, avoiding my eyes.

'*You* don't have visitors,' I corrected. 'I heard your new husband has plenty.'

'What do *you* know?! Who've you been speaking to?"

'Nothing. No-one. I thought you were entertaining last weekend, that's all.'

'Hardly entertaining. Standing there like a mannequin whilst the neighbours nosed around my home and -' She stopped herself as if suddenly aware that she'd said too much.

'You do have an eye for lovely things, Jess.' I said, trying to lighten the mood. 'I got twenty quid for that belt you brought in last month.'

She balked. 'Twenty pounds for a Hermes belt? It's worth ten times that!'

'People aint gonna pay that down the pubs,' I laughed. God, she was so out of touch these days.

She didn't reply but she lifted the sunglasses up onto her head and smiled apologetically. Her make-up was thick but, this close up, I could see the dark circles under her eyes.

'You're forgetting how things are for the rest of us,' I chastised. 'How they used to be for you.' She finished her water and picked up her bag.

'I must dash Kim. I need to get back for…you know.'

'I know,' I said, saving her from any explanation. 'I'll see ya. Second Wednesday of the month?'

'Maybe,' I frowned at that answer. 'I mean yes,' she corrected. 'Yes, I'll be here. Try and get here on time, will you?' She left then, without a goodbye. I didn't turn around. I went straight to my backpack. She'd done well for me this time and taken my advice to stick to small, girlie stuff. If I shifted it this afternoon I'd have enough money to settle the balance on Jayden's school trip.

'Ere! Your posh mate ordered this for you,' said Fat Sam, putting a full English down in front of me. 'Tried to pay with a bloody card! A card! I said it's cash or no breakfast, lady.'

'She's not my mate,' I said. 'She's my little sister.'

*

I pulled out of The Fox's carpark quickly, glad for my tinted windows. I waited until I was a mile away before taking my sunglasses off. Sitting at some traffic lights, I noticed that my fingers were tapping the wheel and my knee was bouncing up and down. I rolled my shoulders and tried to relax into my seat.

My earlier good mood had deserted me. The buzz I got from my little shopping trips never lasted long. Perhaps that's why I kept doing it. I wasn't bored. I wasn't hormonal. I definitely wasn't some attention-seeking housewife hoping to be caught doing something naughty. Besides, I wouldn't be caught, I was too good. Too experienced.

There was a time, not all that long ago, when the snooty sales assistants would look down their cosmetically contoured noses at me. No one sprayed me with samples then. Now I had Malcolm's store cards in my purse and those girls were like stink on shit. The sycophantic fools deserved to be robbed.

It was that dingy pub that had soured my mood. I hated its peeling walls and itchy seats. I hated the awkward exchanges with Kim and I was starting to hate her too. The remark about not having an invite was bothering me most. She'd not shown an interest before, she knew the deal. It didn't fit my new image to have a chavvy sister and her stroppy kid in the family. Much better to be an orphan with no living relatives.

Kim and me, we both do what's necessary to get by. That's how I ended up married to Malcolm. I've not forgotten my roots though. I've always taken care of my sister, since we were kids. And despite my recent 'orphan' status, I've seen to it that her and Jayden have been alright. I even had plans to move them off that awful estate eventually but Sally's snooping shut down that possibility.

She is always turning up, like Columbo, with her downcast demeanour and seemingly innocent but endless questions. I'd caught her fishing around for a binned receipt once and when her weekly dusting of Malcolm's study became almost daily, I'd decided it was

12

too risky to use his accounts to support Kim. That's when I slipped back into my old line of work. It's a means to an end, like it's always been.

So, I have Sally's snooping to contend with and now Kim is threatening to put my new life at risk. It occupied my thoughts all the way home and I arrived back with no knowledge of the drive there.

I could smell lasagne, Malcolm's favourite, when I let myself in. Sally had laid out the marble breakfast bar with the place settings and I poured myself a glass from the wine sitting in the cooler. She fussed with a salad but I could feel her watching me.

'Well, I'll be off shortly. I'm seeing my son this afternoon,' she said.

'Don't let me keep you,' I took a sip from my glass. The crisp wine was delicious.

'You might know him, Jessica.'

'I doubt it,' I said. *Just let me enjoy my wine, woman.*

'Works over Old Fox Hill way. Runs a pub down there. Name's Sam.' She stared at me and I took a gulp of my wine, my eyes fixed on the view from the patio doors.

'Not an area I'm familiar with. Here's

Malcolm,' I said, hearing his tyres on the gravel. 'No need for you to serve Sally, I'll do it.' I took the salad bowl from her but she didn't move.

'Such a generous man,' she said. 'Always been kind to my family, has Malcolm, at Christmas and what not.'

'Yes well, don't let me keep you. I'll dish this out,' the salad bowl threatened to crack as my grip on it tightened.

'Always an invite for us to his little shindigs. He used to have lots of them. I've never accepted of course,' her expression was passive but she didn't take her eyes off me.

'Makes sense not to mix business with pleasure,' I replied and swapped the bowl for my wine glass. Sally took a small step towards me.

' It just didn't seem right,' she continued. 'And I've been a bit embarrassed of my humble background. But do you know, I'll take him up on the next one! No reason me and my Sam wouldn't fit in. *You* have.'

I stepped around her, pushed the patio doors open and went outside, gulping in the fresh air. Malcom entered the kitchen then. He said something I couldn't hear and they both laughed, Sally's laugh too loud and too long.

I drained the contents of my glass, fixed my smile in place and went back inside. 'Hello love, good game?'

'Not my best today,' Malcolm answered and he launched into a tale about his morning on the golf course. I smiled and nodded, hearing none of it. My eyes were following Sally as she served out the lasagne and tidied the last few things away.

'You can manage the dishwasher can't you Jessica?' she asked, loading a few dishes into it.

'Yes, Sally I'm quite capable of that.'

'Very good. I'll let myself in at seven tomorrow. I'll prepare breakfast early as I've some paperwork to catch up on. Online ordering and whatnot.'

'Don't know what I'd do without you keeping me organised,' said Malcolm.

'Just doing my job,' Sally flashed him a big smile. 'See you both tomorrow.'

Malcolm sat down to his lunch but I was rooted to the spot, my arms by my sides and fists clenched. Sally gathered her things and left. On her way out, she adjusted the arrangement of lilies on the table, looked back over her shoulder at me, and smiled.

ABOVE AVERAGE

Trigger Warning: References suicide.

Quiet. Nice. Average. These are some of the words that were scrawled on the yellow sticky notes that my colleagues have stuck to the front of my buttoned up white blouse. We are at our first ever team building day and the lively facilitator has directed us to write down one-word descriptions of each other.

'This is a safe space, guys. Let's all be really, really honest with each other,' she encourages.

'Safe enough for me to share what's on my camera roll from last Friday night?' shouts one of the I.T lads and the rest of the group laughs. I smile tightly but I've no idea what he's joking about. I hadn't gone along to the after-work drinks last week or any week, come to think of it.

Perhaps that is why they think I'm quiet. But average? That hurts. You can't really get to know anyone in our white-washed, hive of cubicles. There is an uninterrupted buzz of low level activity as we type, stamp and scrawl away. The occasional pollination at the printer is no time at all to get to know anyone. I quite like it like that, the anonymity of being a small part of a big machine.

But this team building day really has me

doubting myself. Doubting my place in the world even. I spend my journey home, considering how people really see me. I mull it over all night and see every passing hour flick over on my alarm clock. It is with a sense of dread that I set off for work the next morning so it is all the more remarkable that shortly after, I try to stop someone from jumping from a railway bridge.

I'm waiting for the 07:59 from Somerton. It's a small, redbrick station, which is yet to catch up with the advent of self-service machines and automatic barriers. It's quite busy in rush hour and the resident busker probably does well, despite the melancholy mood of his musical choices.

There are just two platforms, each with a tiny waiting room where the commuters cram in on cold days. The green plastic seats are hard and worn and there are just five of them, so on milder days everyone hovers outside.

The weather is miserable so I squeeze into the packed, waiting room and end up right against the door. Rain is beating against it and the glass pane rattles from frequent blasts of wind. Then I see him, he's impossible to miss, balanced up on Somerton Bridge. I quickly glance around but no one is reacting, their attention is sucked into tiny screens. So I start moving, with no knowledge of what I intend to do. I spill out of the stifling closeness of the waiting room and into the freezing fresh air, splashing across the short platform.

There are steep metal steps which are slippy on a damp day and downright lethal on a tempestuous day like this one but I somehow make it swiftly up onto the bridge. The bridge itself is made up of metal panels which were once a deep blue but are now a mix of graffiti, gunge and bodily fluids. There is a railing along the top and it is here that the guy is sitting.

He is dressed in dark jeans, a black puffa jacket and trainers and he is hunched over so tightly that his shoulders frame his ears. There is nothing distinctive about him and later, when the Transport Police ask me, I will say that he was a 'thirty-something, white male, of average build'.

My auto-pilot snaps off as suddenly as it had come on and I find myself in the centre of the bridge, clinging onto the railings like an upset toddler in a cot. I hate heights. My laptop bag is abandoned at my feet, my long hair is soaking and my raincoat is whipped around me like cling-film. I want to sweep my hair out of my eyes but I daren't let go.

I take a good look at him. The jeans are worn and dirty and the puffa jacket is sagging like an old duvet. He is sitting atop the railings with his feet hooked around them. I can see his bare ankles, the frayed hems of his jeans not quite meeting the tops of a pair of ageing trainers.

Beneath his soaking brown curls is a blank, wet face. The rain runs in rivulets down his cheeks but he is expressionless, his brown eyes staring out at something I can't see.

He is sitting with his hands clasped together on his lap. They are bright pink from the cold and there is a thin gold band on his left ring finger. My own gloved hands are, I'm sure, white from the tightness of my grip. But for his precarious position, he might have been meditating. I see all of this like a movie trailer, the details flashing through my consciousness in seconds.

With the next gust of wind, he sways. I gasp and squeeze my eyes shut. When I open them, he is still there, unblinking.

A crowd has gathered somewhere close. Maybe the steps. Maybe even on the bridge itself. I'd sensed it a few moments ago but I didn't want to look away from him. There is shouting but the wind muffles any words before they reach us.

My stomach is doing the salsa as I take a few tentative steps towards him. I've no idea what to say, what would be helpful. I begin babbling and several seconds pass before I realise that he can't hear me. I edge closer, my hands never once leaving the railing.

'What's your name?' I call but he doesn't respond. 'It's not safe up here. Please. Come down.'

He seems unaware of my presence so I try again, 'Let me help you down. I want to help you.'

'You've never wanted to help before. Piss off and leave me alone!' The force of his venomous tone causes me to step back, straight into a puddle. My ballet flats are soaked.

'Let's go inside. You can tell me how I can help,' I hear myself say but what I'm thinking is, 'Please someone, come up here and help us both.'

He ignores me. In the distance, I see the cross-country train. It doesn't stop at Somerton but thunders through at 07:53.

'Please,' I say feebly. And then, like a child learning to dive, he clumsily pushes off from his seated position. Head down, eyes closed, arms outstretched.

I jerk my head away and my ears catch the long, loud horn of the train. A noise escapes from my throat. I feel it, rather than hear it - a short, guttural outburst that leaves me limp. I don't look down. I can't look down. Instead, I turn my face skyward into the rain and close my eyes.

Whilst up on the bridge, time had raced by but in the little staff room, behind the ticket office, it was crawling. There is a large clock above the door and I watch its black hands play tag lazily over Roman numerals.

The ticks and tocks are accompanied by chart music from a radio somewhere in the room and this auditory cocktail is sprinkled with outbursts from the station tannoy. I feel drunk and not good drunk.

I see my wet coat draped over a radiator on the opposite side of the room and I realise that I am wrapped in an oversized, green fleece. It smells of Brut and cigarettes but I don't mind. My teeth are chattering so I reach for the steaming mug on the table beside me but I can't grip it. Instead, I concertina myself, tucking my hands under my armpits to stop them from shaking.

It is strange being in this room, seeing a new layer of a place I thought I knew well. It's windowless and musty with a single bulb hanging, naked, from an artexed ceiling. There are crinkled, yellowing notices tacked haphazardly onto every wall and a vintage Page Three is taped inside the door of an open locker in the corner.

'Wasn't expecting company, sorry,' says a portly man who I hadn't noticed. He slams the locker shut and leans against it. He is wearing a uniform, minus his fleece.

A middle-aged man bends over me, his wide brow a labyrinth of deep grooves. He is saying something but I don't quite hear what. My attention is back on the noise of the clock and the radio. And that horn.

He places his large hands on my shoulders and leans in; close enough that I can smell his coffee breath. His touch is grounding. I shift my head away slightly and notice the logo on his chest and the epaulettes on his shoulder.

'- some questions, love.' He gives me a gentle shake.

'Sorry? What?'

'I'm going to have to ask you some questions,' the constable repeats.

'He said I never wanted to help before.'

The constable looks across the room at the other man who shrugs. 'It's the shock, love. Is there someone you'd like me to call?'

'There's no one. He said I never wanted to help.' I had been searching around in the recesses of my memory but still didn't recognise the man who had jumped. I was certain that I did not know him but his words had left me feeling uneasy.

'Well I've a few questions then we'll get you home.' The constable takes a slim notebook out of his pocket and pulls a chair up beside me. The sound of the metal legs dragging along the floor is auditory overload. I weep.

When we arrive outside my modest maisonette later that day, the kind man from the Transport Police holds the car door open for me, then walks me to my front door.

'I really should call someone for you. How about your fella?'

'I'm single. And I'm fine. Really'

'Your folks then. You've had a rough morning.'

'Honestly I'm fine but thanks anyway.' I offer him a weak smile and he heads back to his car with a mock salute.

A long breath escapes me. There is a pulsing in my temples which is threatening to spread behind my eyes. I quickly let myself in, run a deep bath and stay in it until I am shrunken. Then I climb into bed and flick the TV onto the late lunchtime news. I don't think I even make it past the headlines.

It is the small hours of the next morning when I wake up. I have three pleasant seconds before I remember that I had watched a man jump to his death. I stay cocooned within my duvet and stare up at the ceiling. I can't sleep, can't read, can't do anything besides replay earlier events.

My alarm is scheduled for six am and I always head straight out for a run. Today I snooze the alarm twice and on the third alert, I fling the little black clock across the room. The batteries clatter against the wooden floor and roll under my bed.

When I eventually get up, I swipe through the local news sites and social media accounts whilst nursing a strong black coffee. One single tweet acknowledges the events of yesterday:

08:04 RT @LocalLink Passengers warned of significant delays due to trespasser on the line at

*#Somerton All services expected to resume after 11am .
#traveldelays #crosscity*

     I stare miserably into my wardrobe, at a barcode
of black trousers and white blouses. Then, on impulse, I
find myself delving into the far end where the clothes
I'm gifted each Christmas by my younger sister, hang
with the tags still on. Bright and tight is her motto.

     As I dress, I listen to the local news but there is
no mention of the Somerton jumper. I don't know what
I was expecting but the absence of any report of him
leaves me feeling angry. He is reduced to a trespasser,
forgotten after one hundred and twenty characters.

     On my way out, my mobile phone beeps. *Happy
Birthday love, call round later? XXX Dad.* I stop short,
momentarily confused. I had completely forgotten the
date. There isn't time to text back, there's a stop I need
to make before catching the train.

As I walk to the station I catch my reflection in a
window. Looking back at me is a woman in a striking
red coat, tottering a little unsteadily in heels. A large,
flat box of cakes and pastries is balanced across one arm
and a muddied laptop bag hangs from the crook of the
other.

I turn into the entrance and try to ignore the sudden hollowing in my stomach and tightening in my throat. It seems quieter than usual, the atmosphere is muted somehow.

As I paused to check the departure board there was a voice beside me. 'Wasn't sure if you'd be here today.' A familiar mix of Brut and tobacco invades my nostrils.

'I have to go to work. I'm a bit late though.'

'Almost didn't recognise you. You alright? You know, after... after yesterday.'

'I think so, yes.'

'Best to get straight back on the horse, and all that,' He nods at me and strolls away.

Whilst waiting, I stare at the platform directly opposite until my sore eyes water. It is an effort not to look up at the bridge and when the train arrives I am already over the yellow line, my finger poised to jab at the button on the doors.

I look out of the window as the train draws away and it is then that the cause of the quietness occurs to me. The guitarist, a homeless busker, was missing from his usual spot. He hadn't been there yesterday either.

SEEN TO BE DONE

Brian

'Will the court stand please.' It is not a request, it's an order. The murmurs and hushed conversations are immediately shushed as if turned off by a tap. There is a wave of movement as everyone rises to their feet, waiting to play their part in proceedings.

I've enjoyed giving that order for nearly thirty years. I always take a sip of water from my plastic cup first and then say it, in what I like to think is my commanding voice. It's the same voice I use when there's argy-bargy outside the court-room doors or when Barbara wants to book another cruise on our overdraft.

It's not me saying it today though, it's Andrea. A wispy haired, stick insect with a pout. Looks about seventeen. I've been training her up but I'm not sure she'll last. There's an art to being an usher, it takes…presence.

'There's an awful row on the landing,' she said to me a few months into her training. 'Security is tied up downstairs and no one's listening to me.'

I'm not surprised no one listens to her, with that silly fringe hanging in front of her eyes. I'd marched out, black gown flapping behind me, armed only with

my clipboard and a biro. I'd expected a brawl judging
by Andrea's hand wringing. Instead, I found a scruffy
young couple who had clearly spent the lunch period
lubricating their lies in the pub next door and were now
having a heated disagreement about whose alibi was
most plausible.

'Unless you two want your case put to the back
of the list, you better pipe down!' I'd yelled. Punch and
Judy soon slumped back into the blue plastic seats,
scowling.

It used to be a contempt of court to come in
stinking of booze. Security would send for me and I'd
have them up in front of the bench sharpish. But that
was a long time ago. Now they get an arched eyebrow
from the Legal Advisor when they come staggering in
and an ATR from the lefty chairman.

That's an Alcohol Treatment Requirement, for
the uninitiated. When you've worked in court rooms as
long as I have, you can't help using the lingo. If you
could get a law degree by osmosis, I'd be giving Perry
Mason a run for his money.

Andrea had scurried back into court behind me,
shaking her head and looking concerned. She doesn't
like it when I get loud with the defendants. She thinks

we should cajole and counsel the troublemakers, try to keep them calm before they come in for their case but I'm not a bloody social worker.

She's had months of training but this work can't be taught from a laminated handout or a workshop on diversity. You learn *on* the job. So, it's her facilitating the proceedings today. She went bright red when she told everyone to stand and she's not given me eye contact once.

We're in court four of the Crown Court today. It isn't like the Magistrate's Court, which is where I usually work. The Crown is nice and traditional, a glass dock, green leather seats, the bench up on a dais and an earthy smell, like old books. It's a lovely looking building.

The Magistrate's court across the street has been converted so it's all flat screen monitors and an open-plan look to appear accessible. But I don't think courts should be accessible, they should scare the bejesus out of people, then maybe they'll stay out of trouble.

The Legal Advisor's fingertips didn't even leave her keyboard when she rose. Bright red false nails and they clickety-clack something terrible. The sound goes right through me, makes me want to rip the silly things off her fingers. Barbara wears her nails like that too. Never done a day's typing in her life though.

The solicitors, sorry, advocates we call them now. The advocates are leaning towards each other, whispering. One of them, Mr Snell, is wearing a ridiculous, canary-yellow bow tie. Thinks it makes him look quirky but he looks like Mr Blobby. He's no respect at all for the dress code. 'Sombre attire' is what we're meant to wear. There was a play I read once, *Murmuring Judges* I think it was. One character says to the other 'I can't hear you, your trousers are too loud.' They'd be deafened by this fellow.

Alan from probation is the only one to look at me directly and he looks knackered. He's getting on, is Al. Can't afford to retire yet though, much like me. Nice bloke. We used to have a pint next door on a Friday afternoon. It's been a while since we did that.

So, here we are. Each of us is in our marked positions, like a team waiting for kick off. Then a hidden door opens in a wood panelled wall and out traipses the Judge.

It's always a bit anti-climatic, watching the Judge shuffle along to his seat on the platform. You expect something grand but usually it's just a middle-aged bloke, same as me except for the daft wig.

I fancied myself as a lay judge, years back, even sent off for the forms but you don't get paid for being a Magistrate and that put me right off. Voluntary work is not conducive to my Barbara's mounting store card bills and endless home improvements.

The Judge pours himself into a riveted leather chair which sits directly beneath a huge coat of arms, then he nods, indicating that everyone can sit. Everyone except me that is. When you're in the dock, you stay standing until you're told to be seated.

Technically, I'm not in the dock. I was during my trial but that was weeks ago. Today is my sentencing hearing so I'm sitting on the third row of benches with my advocate, behind Mr Blobby from the CPS.

Andi

It was ever so awkward, listening to Mr Snell talk about Brian. It's ok for him, this is just another case. When it's all over he'll go back to CPS Towers and on to his next case but I can't do that.

I've been dreading today for weeks. Ever since the guilty verdict came through, things have been dead weird at work. Brian hasn't been here of course, part of his bail conditions was that he must keep away from the Court House. But he *is* here. In the fabric of the place, like a lingering smell that permeated the walls.

My fella says I should just keep my head down and concentrate on doing a good job. He says it's a job for life and I'll soon forget all the fuss but I'm not convinced. Mud sticks and with Brian being my mentor, people have been a bit funny with me.

I'd booked annual leave this week so as to stay out of it all but with sickness and whatnot, here I am. I finished my training months ago but I'm usually across the road in the Magistrate's. This is only my third time in the Crown Court and I've the added pressure of Brian being here. It's making me nervous.

Even in his...predicament, he's been watching me, back straight and stubbled chin pointed up. I didn't give him the satisfaction of returning his gaze but from the side of my eye, I've seen him follow me around the room, checking on the way I'm doing things.

On my first day, when he'd been assigned as my mentor, the first thing he'd said was 'You're not Andy. I'm expecting an Andy. Andy Morton.' He'd referred to his clipboard and given me a disapproving look.

Well hello to you too Mister, I'd wanted to say but instead I'd said, 'I'm Andrea but everyone calls me Andi. Andy with an I.'

'Everyone's not working for Her Majesty's court service, Andrea.' He had a lofty way of speaking, like a Headteacher dealing with a first-former.

'Er...no. Yeah,' I said. I wasn't sure how to respond so I trotted out my usual joke. 'My Dad thought my Mum was having a boy,' I explained and I gave a little laugh but he stared at me stony faced. I suppose that first interaction set the tone for the rest of our relationship, despite my efforts to get along.

His wife, Barbara, is here today. I met her once, way before all of this. Brian and me were outside on a fag break and she pulled up in a new car, waving his lunchbox.

'I don't know why he had me come all the way over here,' she said to me. 'He could have easily grabbed something from in town.'

'Waste of money. Homemade sandwiches will do me,' Brian said. 'I imagine you'll be lunching out with one of your ladies from the Health Club again.'

She seemed a nice enough woman and she paid little attention to his remarks, rolling her eyes

36

dramatically for my benefit. We'd both giggled but I soon shut up when I saw Brian's face. He didn't speak to me for the rest of the day. He was moody like that.

He was a good usher though. Efficient and respected, if not particularly liked. He was a stickler for the rules and there was nothing about the system that he didn't know. That's why it's so shocking to see him here like this. I wasn't in court for his trial but I heard all about it. The rest of the staff talked about nothing else for weeks.

At one point, I was questioned by the Police and investigated internally too. I was convinced that I would fail my probation. HR said I must have been involved, what with us working so closely together. They said if I told them everything I knew, there would be no charges and I could resign before I was sacked. I did tell them everything and the investigation into me was quickly dropped.

I get no satisfaction from seeing him up in front of the bench even though I played a part in putting him there. I go over to the gallery and do a cursory check that no one is using a phone but it's just to occupy myself really, I hate all the standing around.

I don't usually have to check the gallery. Apart

from the next defendant to be called, it's usually empty. Today though, the four rows of worn leather seats have people packed together like matchsticks. Barbara is on the front row. Our eyes meet and I offer her a weak smile but she doesn't return it.

'We need more copies of the PSR please, Miss Morton.' The Legal Advisor is looking at me expectantly.

'Er…yes. They're on the court store, Madam Clerk.'

'His Honour prefers a hard copy, rather than the iPad,' she says and then under her breath 'Luddite.'

'I'll go and run some copies off,' I say. Brian hates the court iPads, says they'll do us out of our jobs. He'd be livid if he'd heard the Clerk mocking the Judge.

When I return, Alan from probation is already summing up what his team has put into the pre-sentence report. He's nervous and the Judge has to ask him to keep his voice up. I glance at Brian. He's leaning forward, his chin resting on his interlocked hands, in that way of his that appears like he's listening intently but he's not. His solicitor will have shown him that report already, he's just trying to put Alan off.

'Mrs Bains,' the Judge says, nodding at Brian's

solicitor. She rises slowly. She's got her work cut out if you ask me. Misconduct in a public office usually leads to custody.

Brian

Maleficence Mr Snell called it. I rather like that word. It has an air of importance to it. If you've got to have a stain on your record, an unblemished record at that, then you want something like a maleficence. It rather sets you apart from the toe rags who defraud the taxman or the bums claiming benefits they're not entitled to. Lord knows I've seen enough of them pass through here. Bloody awful the lot of them.

Mr Snell did his best to make me look like a hardened criminal. I was minded to correct him a few times but I wouldn't sink so low as to embarrass myself with a contempt of court on my record.

I've no doubt they'll make an example of me. The proverbial book must be thrown and I'm in its line of fire. It's only right and proper I suppose.

Mrs Bains advised me to plead guilty. She was the duty solicitor at the police station on that awful day when I was brought in for questioning. She told me straight away to come clean. I believe the phrase she used was 'bang to rights.'

'No such thing,' I'd told her. 'A man has the right to be judged by a jury of his peers.' I knew right then, despite the evidence, that I'd take my chances. I've seen enough cases in my time to know that evidence has very little to do with it. The CPS mess up so often, it's embarrassing and cases frequently collapse.

My case didn't collapse though. The CPS did their job and they did it rather well I thought. Mrs Bains did her best for me in her mitigation statement today but she was no match for Mr Snell. He'd have real gravitas if he wore a proper tie.

She went for the emotional jugular, a technique I've seen used successfully many times. She said I was a man of good character , a church man with a wife who depended on him. The Court is wary of coming down too hard on people whom others rely on or who are turning their life around. Rehabilitation, not punishment, that's the way things are going. Though not for me I don't think. His Honour doesn't look too impressed with me at all.

Barbara is here. I've always thought defendant's look much more respectable with a supportive family in the public gallery. She could have turned the volume down on her snivelling though, it's quite distracting. The tears aren't for me, she's only upset for herself. It's the guilt.

She's the reason I'm in this bit of bother. Decorating, shopping, holidays… it was constant. She's an addict. A lip-sticked, designer-bag carrying version of the shaking, sweating, thieving lot I've seen many times in my career. I should have left her. I thought about it many times but solicitors are so expensive.

I play the organ at St. Peter's, fifteen years this summer. Barbara does the teas after service every Sunday. Divorce would not have looked good at all and I couldn't have had our finances being the talk of the parish. Our home is really quite beautiful. She does have an eye for interior design, does my Barbara, I'll give her that but I expect we'll lose the house very soon.

She went to debt counselling two years ago and I took out another loan. A big one. We were getting straightened out financially, hadn't had a holiday in months and then she discovered online bingo. Before I knew it, bailiffs were taking everything they could carry. I needed to make extra money before we lost everything.

His Honour has gone to lunch now. Then we'll be back to see what's to be done with me. I wonder if young Andrea can vacate us all from the room in an orderly fashion. Half-soaked and half-asleep most of the time, that one.

Andi

I'm so glad for the recess but I make the decision to not go into the staff room, I'd rather be on my own for a bit. I potter around the courtroom instead, clearing up plastic cups, chewed up pens and scraps of paper. We're supposed to be digital and for the most part we are but there is always paper of some sort to be dealt with. I gather it up and place it in a pile on my seat, for shredding later.

'All these letters after their names but they're bloody careless,' Brian would moan whilst he tidied up. He was right about the solicitors being lax but I thought it was odd, him lowering himself to a simple task that he could delegate to me. But he insisted, he said it wasn't just paper, it was the 'business of the court' and needed to be in capable hands.

It was several weeks into my training when I realised that he would sometimes take the papers home. I said nothing when I saw a few folded sheets sticking out of his back pocket one afternoon. I said nothing

42

when I saw him take a snap on his phone once. I said nothing for months, putting it down to one of his many idiosyncrasies.

There were lots of unusual things that he did. Nothing significant on their own but added together…just strange. Like his breaks, they always had to be at a set time and if he was excused late he'd be all twitchy and dash off.

He was always looking at his phone too, though I can't imagine there'd be any apps on an ancient thing like the one he had. I wondered if he had a fancy woman. It would explain why he was always so rude about his wife.

'Couldn't be getting on with one of those posh, touch screen things you young people are using,' he'd told me, stuffing the relic into his inside pocket when he caught me looking once. I could swear that every so often, the phone changed too.

Warrant applications were where he really got weird, though it took some time for me to realise it. Once I'd got to grips with things and knew my way around, I started to notice a bit of a pattern. Whenever there were warrants to be heard, Brian would juggle things so that they ended up on our court list and not another usher's.

It's all a bit cloak and dagger when the Police come to apply for a warrant. There are only a select few allowed inside the courtroom; the legal advisor, a single Magistrate and the usher. Or in our case, two ushers – me in training.

The Police will outline why they are applying for a warrant and what intelligence they have gathered. They have all these codes to grade the intelligence, E1 this and B2 that. Like the numbers on a chocolate wrapper. It's gobbledy gook to me but Brian seemed to understand it all quite well.

Sometimes the Magistrate will ask a couple of questions before deciding whether or not to grant the application but the Police don't tell them how or when the warrant will be executed, that's all classified. It could be days or sometimes only hours later when the Police descend on their suspect. We never know.

There's not much for an Usher to do other than make sure that no one enters the room. I found the warrant applications quite boring and much preferred to be in the trial courts but Brian seemed very interested. Like I said, strange man.

He would sometimes slip off to make calls

afterwards. He'd leave me with some mickey mouse task for my 'personal development' and then he'd be straight off to the Usher's admin office. If the office was busy, he'd nip out, motioning to me that I was to stay inside.

I thought it was quite cheeky that he gave himself extra breaks and denied me the same privilege but the more I got to know him, the more I realised that wasn't his style. He wasn't taking breaks, he was up to something he didn't want me to know.

One of the first things Brian ever taught me was the importance of being attentive. 'We are the eyes and ears of this place, Andrea,' he said. 'If you want your court to run smoothly, stay alert.' And that's exactly what I did do. I listened and I learned and I watched. I watched *all* the time. I watched Brian and then I blew the whistle.

I had to. The sanctity of the court must be respected. Brian taught me that himself. So, I went to the bosses with my suspicions. They told me that my concerns had been noted, I was to return to my duties and say nothing. They were already onto him, though I didn't know it then.

It was the dummy warrant a few weeks later that

caught him out. The Police applied to raid a grow house and destroy cannabis plants with a street value of thirty thousand pounds. Brian was up to his usual, except this time there was no grow house. It was a dummy warrant. The Police had found their leak.

Tip-offs. That's what he'd been doing. Counterfeit goods, anti-social pubs, that sort of thing. And drugs too, though Mrs Bains was keen to make the point that it was cannabis and Spice - not the hard stuff. Brian drew the line there. His logic was that there was no harm done if the odd seller of knock-off fags got a head-start in moving their gear elsewhere. He'd tip them off, they'd clear out before the Police arrived and then a brown envelope would end up in Brian's palm. He'd been at it for months.

It took me a while to prove that I hadn't been in on it with him. Brian could have spoken up for me and cleared the whole matter up in minutes but he didn't. He simply denied all the allegations and didn't comment about me at all.

I was so relieved when the matter was dropped and I passed my probation. Things have been better since Brian was suspended. I enjoy my job now and I think I'm going to be really good at it.

Brian

I've seen the prisoner transport vans outside the courthouse many times but this is my first time inside one. It's ever so poky. There are six of us in all, in little compartments squashed together. The cuffs on my wrists are digging into me and the seat is too low down for my long legs, so it's impossible to get comfy. It reeks of body odour too. These young men should take more pride in themselves. I do hope it's not a long drive.

I'm still in my suit but the guard has taken my tie, belt and shoelaces, so I'm not looking my best. I'm glad for the tinted windows. There were quite a few photographers outside court when the van pulled away.

Mrs Bains says I can appeal today's decision but I'll need to find someone else to represent me as her caseload is full for the foreseeable. I don't think I'll bother.

Not only must justice be done, it must be *seen* to be done. The system must have legitimacy in order to be respected and there's no question that I bought it into disrepute. I do worry though. We're already short staffed and now the team will be another one down with me going away.

Andrea will have to step up. I suppose she didn't do too badly today. Lacking in attention to detail some of the time but overall, she had a good command of the room and was very vigilant. She might actually go places but of course, she's had a good teacher.

DADDY'S GIRL

'No. Stop. Put it back,' demanded the old woman.

'You're doing it all wrong and you'll break it with those oars of yours.'

Janet glanced at her pale, pudgy hands, a yellow dust cloth in the right, a Royal Doulton figurine in the left.

'Mother, you said you wanted me to -'

'I know what I said but you're not doing it right. They're fragile, you idiot!'

Janet looked down at the pink carpet, which was freshly vacuumed, and chewed her bottom lip. Her eyes followed the lines in the thick pile. It reminded her of a freshly cut lawn, the way her dad used to do it with the stripes.

'I don't suppose you've tidied up the kitchen.'

Janet sighed. 'I have. It's spotless. It's always spotless.'

'Well don't stand there dawdling. Get off to work.' Then more quietly, 'Alan must be turning in his grave.'

'What?' Janet's head snapped up on hearing her father's name.

'You should be looking after me, not moping

about making the place look untidy. I don't get a minute's peace with having to always have one eye on you. Probably why his heart gave out in the first place. He was always worrying about you.'

A tiny speck of blood appeared on Janet's bottom lip and she licked it away. The duster fell to the floor and the knuckles of her other hand went white.

*

A steady stream of ticket holders passed through the station concourse, autopilot carrying them to their platforms and onto their trains. Most were focussed on their phones. Eyes down for a full house of likes, shares and retweets.

The closed shutters of the ticket office went unnoticed until an elderly couple arrived. The gentleman frowned, his eyebrows spelling out a deep 'W'.

'I can't work this flaming timetable out,' he moaned. 'Someone should be here this time of the morning.' He rapped his knuckles on the corrugated metal.

Behind the shutter was a poky, windowless office that smelled of musty books. A teary-eyed Janet had just let herself into it. She placed her belongings in her locker and shuffled up to the desk, her grey, polyester slacks making a swish-swish sound as they rubbed together.

She poured herself into a frayed swivel chair and jabbed at the buttons on various bits of equipment. A series of green lights blinked on and a whirring noise started. With shaky fingers, Janet straightened the name badge on her lapel. Then she pressed one last button and the shutters gave a rusty outburst and slowly rolled up. She tucked a stray wisp of greying hair behind her ear and inhaled deeply. This was the first time in thirty-six years that she had been late for work.

'Come on!' someone yelled from the other side of the Perspex. 'That bloody machine is on the blink again and my train is due any minute now.' A short line of irritated commuters had formed behind the elderly couple. Janet swallowed down a sob.

Once she had dealt with the queue, she saw to the ticket machines on the drafty concourse and carried out the daily checks around the station. Winter wasn't far away and she was glad to retreat back to the office where a convector heater rattled beneath her desk.

Soon, dark circles had appeared under her arms but she didn't turn the heat down. Her mother rarely allowed the heating at home to be switched on. Waste of money apparently. Jumpers and blankets sufficed before central heating was invented and they'd still suffice now. So Janet liked to make the most of the warmth at work.

There were no trains due for a while, so she retrieved a Mills & Boon from her locker and settled down. After a few minutes, she realised she had been reading the same page over and over and she tossed the book onto the desk. She was thinking of the horrible things her mother had said that morning and she was thinking about her dad. He had been on her mind a lot lately.

He'd worked at the station as a signaller when Janet was just a girl. Each day after school, she and her younger siblings would count the passing fast trains whilst waiting for him to get off work. Then they'd walk the mile home together.

As soon as she had left school, Janet had got a job at the same station, as a junior. She had made tea, kept the office tidy and learned the timetables by rote. Her dad was delighted to have her around the place.

A serious back injury had brought him to a premature retirement. Then the heart problems started and he had eventually become house-bound. He lived vicariously through Janet and when she had become a station assistant he was thrilled.

'You'll make management love,' he'd said, but her mother had disagreed.

'Our Janet in management?' she had scoffed. 'She'd never cope! Besides, we can't have her swanning about the network. She's needed at home.'

Briefly, the younger Janet had dared to dream. She had lived in Conberton all her life. A tiny place. A promotion would mean travel, new people, perhaps even someone special. Her mother had been right though, Janet had never made management. She had never had the courage to apply.

Single, childless and still living in the family home, it was too late for her now, as her mother liked to remind her often. Her brother and sister had both married young and moved many miles away. The visits at Christmas and birthdays had dwindled to hastily scrawled cards in the post. Janet couldn't remember the last time she'd seen them.

'The kids don't want to be stuck in that old house,' her sister had explained. 'Come to us this year Jan, do you good to get away for a few days.'

Janet had rebuffed the offer. 'You know I can't

leave Dad. Mother doesn't know his meds and stuff.'

'Mother doesn't need to when she's got you running around like a blue-arsed fly but suit yourself.'

Janet had considered moving to be closer to them but her mother had made her feel terribly guilty for even suggesting it.

'You're needed here. At home. I can't lift Alan by myself so don't go getting any grand ideas.' So that was that. Janet had worked and she had taken care of the house and her dad. One year rolled into another and here she was.

At lunchtime she put the shutter down, unwedged herself from her chair and withdrew an old leather briefcase from her locker. It was a faded shade of brown and barely visible was the embossed outline of her dad's initials. The case contained a BLT on thick white bread, two cans of coke and a family sized bag of crisps. Janet ate it all.

There was little else to do after that. Being a small station there were few passengers outside of rush hour and even fewer staff. There was Ken, who worked the opposite shift and an ever-changing roster of cleaners from an agency.

Janet didn't mind working alone. The regulars

passed through the station without seeing her and the visitors would come with a query then quickly disappear. That left her with long stretches to read her books and enjoy the peace and quiet.

But lately those long stretches were time to overthink and when she thought for too long, it wasn't good for her. She thought about the things she hadn't done, the opportunities that had passed her by but mostly, she thought about her dad.

His death had not been unexpected but it had still been a blow. Janet found herself sleepwalking through her days now, missing her confidant and cheerleader. Right through his illness and up unto his death, he had always been interested in even the most banal details of her day.

'Here. How many late trains today Jan?' he'd wheeze.

'Three, Dad.'

'Cross country?

'Yep.'

'That'll cost 'em dearly. Wotsit again? We pay away?'

'Delay repay.'

'Same thing.'

Her mother had hated this. She had always resented any time they spent together and would bawl at Janet from her armchair downstairs, making demands.

'Best go and see to her Jan,' Dad would say. 'You know how she gets.'

Now her dad was gone and it felt so unfair. He was a good man and he'd been taken away but her mother was still here and she would probably outlive them all, just to spite them!

The rest of the shift passed by slowly and Janet's mood soured further. When Ken arrived to relive her, she was more than melancholy, she was distraught.

'Bloody hell Janet!' joked Ken, 'Who's died?' She didn't respond. She struggled into her coat, lumbered out of the office and headed for home.

Home was an ex-council house on the edge of a housing estate, known by locals as the 'concrete jungle'. Amongst a row of red brick properties, all sporting vertical blinds, was Janet's house. The looped hem of the fussy net curtains, exposed window sills which were crammed with trinkets and ornaments.

From the bottom of the path, Janet could just make out the side of her mother's wing-backed armchair. It was angled so that she could spy on the neighbours unnoticed. Her mother liked to track the whereabouts and habits of the neighbours and then remark upon their declining rates of respectability to Janet.

Janet exhaled a long breath and turned her key in the lock. Her stomach hollowed as she slowly pushed the door open. The chill in the dark hallway matched that of outside and she did not remove her coat. She hung her key on its hook next to her dad's, an assortment of Allen and window keys on a large caretaker's ring. Janet's fingers brushed over them.

She shuffled sideways down the dark hall, careful to avoid the shelves which jutted out like a rock face. They were full with her mother's porcelain dolls.

Her hand hovered over the living room door handle, then she pulled it back. She could hear the raised voices of a chat show on the TV. Her mother watched them day and night.

Janet decided to make a brew before facing her mother so she went to the kitchen. She stared out of the window as the kettle boiled but saw only her reflection and that of the neat, bleached room.

She looked at her face for a long time. She had her dad's eyes but not his twinkle and her mother's nose and thin, down turned lips. She rarely smiled – her mother had once said she looked demented when she did. Whenever her dad had made her laugh after that, her hand shot up to cover her mouth.

Her mother had stolen any joy they had. She had always been jealous of their closeness but when dad had become seriously ill, she'd made every effort to keep them apart. She would send Janet out on one errand after the other and when those were complete she would have a list of chores around the house to be done. When Dad had finally passed, her mother had remarked,

'Well you've no excuse for hiding upstairs now have you, you lazy cow.'

Janet rinsed her mug out. The clock ticked over to seven o'clock. She squeezed a hard lump down her throat and went to the living room.

Everything was as she had left it. A pile of folded laundry formed a tower of Pisa in one corner, the TV sat blaring in another. The coffee table housed the remote and her mother's cup and saucer.

'Only tradesmen use mugs,' was one of her mother's favourite sayings and a sloth-like smile appeared as Janet thought about the mug she had just left on the drainer.

Her mother's slippered feet were propped up on

a footstool. Her spindly legs were covered with a thick, fluffy blanket and her torso was turned towards the window. The blanket had slipped down to the waist, revealing a tiny frame cocooned in a soft dressing gown. Her usually pinched face was relaxed, the scowl gone, and Janet realised she could not remember when she last saw her mother smile.

At her right temple was a furious, deep gash. Its contents were congealed in her hair and some had snaked a path down her cheek, pooling in the fleecy fabric of her dressing gown. On the floor beside her was a Royal Doulton figurine of a mother and child, a large piece of the base chipped off.

The anxiety of the day suddenly fell away. Janet's breathing slowed and her fingers uncoiled. She knew what she had to do. She would do as she had always done, she would take care of her chores.

She moved silently around the room, drawing the curtains, plumping cushions and collecting her mother's cup. She returned to pick up the pile of laundry, putting it away upstairs.

When everything was as it should be, Janet went quietly downstairs, retrieved her keys and unlocked the front door. Then she sat on the bottom stair, next to the telephone table. As an after-thought she returned to the living room and switched off the TV.   It could be some time before she'd be allowed to return, perhaps not at all. She picked up the phone and dialled 999.

WHITE WALLS

It was late morning when Cat woke from a long, blank sleep. Instinctively she reached out to the bedside table for her smartphone. Her hand grasped like a fairground grabber machine but came back empty. There were no personal phones allowed here.

It was poor timing for a digital detox and she wondered what was happening with the Coleman deal. She had left her husband, Paul, in charge but he was much better suited to being the silent partner in their business. When he visited today, she would tell him to play hard ball or she would check-out and close the deal herself.

She lay amongst the plump pillows feeling guilty for her lie-in but not quite awake enough yet to get going. Someone had already been in and opened the blinds to the French windows, so Cat had full view of a neat garden, overlooked by rooms like her own. She admired the splashes of colour in the raised beds and wished that she could take a quick snap with her phone, to send to her own gardener.

The gardener! She hadn't left instructions for him before going away and there was a diseased apple tree that needed attention. If she was going to stay here any longer, she would need a conference call with Chloe. The idle girl was probably occupied with taking selfies at her desk instead of managing Cat's diary. She felt herself tense up at the thought.

What was it the mindfulness app said? Be present. Be present and count your breaths. Perhaps it was blessings. Count something anyway. She had only ever found the time to listen to it once and that had been at least a year ago.

Cat closed her eyes and tried to enjoy the silence instead. That seemed a mindful thing to do. Only it wasn't silent. Somewhere, outside the window, there were birds. They were chirruping as if in conversation with one another and she pictured them, these unseen birds, having their mothers meeting.

She stifled a rare giggle. *Mother's meeting* had always struck her as an odd phrase. Whenever her late Grandmother had used it, it usually meant the girls had been caught talking instead of doing their chores. '*What meetings do mothers go to,*' the eight-year-old Cat had thought? Forty-year-old Cat was unlikely to find out.

She hated birds, they were vermin. Her own garden attracted lots of them thanks to the feeders that Paul insisted on having.

'I find it therapeutic to watch them. Don't be a spoil sport,' he'd said from behind his binoculars. So Cat had resigned herself to the noisy distraction and kept the patio doors to her home office shut when she was working on weekends. She made a mental note to take down the feeders when she got home, she'd tolerated enough.

No, no mental notes, she reminded herself. She was supposed to be putting her to-do list away for a while. That was the whole point in her being here. Her thoughts drifted back to the Coleman deal.

She weighed up the merits of checking out. It had been a ridiculous idea to take a break now. She needed to get back to work, close the deal and maybe then take some time off. On the other hand, Paul had been insistent that she come away now and she didn't want to appear ungrateful.

She would stay for only a day or two more and suggest a proper holiday together for later in the year. A cruise maybe. Five stars, for a month just like their honeymoon, it would be perfect. But who would manage the business? God, she felt so tired just thinking about it!

The team would just have to manage without

her. She deserved a rest. She *needed* a rest. That was what Paul had said when he'd booked her this little break. Time off. Time out. No mention of time together though.

She would book a massage and try a yoga class out today. Or was it Pilates that they did here? The gazelle-like Chloe did Pilates classes. If she could have a figure like that from some cheap, community instructor, the trainers in this place could surely shape Cat into Madonna.

Perhaps she'd get a little dog once she was home. Then she could take regular walks and get some fresh air. It could be a new project for her and Paul to enjoy together. She'd need Chloe to call the local Dog's Home and some breeders.

She was doing it again. The endless flipping over of the rolodex in her brain. Lists of things to do and arrange. What had happened to the birds? When had they stopped their awful racket? Cat opened her eyes, wondering how anybody ever bothered with this mindfulness thing. It was impossible.

There was a knock at the door then and a friendly-faced woman with a breakfast tray entered without waiting to be invited in. 'Good morning

Catherine. Your breakfast is here,' she said. 'How are you today?'

'I'm ok, Amy. Just set it down there, will you?'

'Some flowers were delivered for you yesterday evening when you were resting. Beautiful they are – white, long stemmed roses. We can't put them in here of course. Glass isn't allowed, you understand. But I bought in the card for you. Here.'

Cat took it from her, immediately recognising Paul's looped scrawl.

'Did he bring them in person?' she asked.

'Who?'

'My husband.'

'No. It was a young woman. Very attractive.'

'Chloe.'

'Your daughter, is she?'

'She's my personal assistant.' Cat dropped the card onto the bed.

'I could do with one of those. I said to my supervisor only yesterday, stick a broom up my-'

'Yes well…thank you, Amy.'

'I'll straighten the room up whilst you eat.'

Cat nodded. Amy was a valuable source of information and with no television in the room, she

provided Cat with some well-needed entertainment.
Whilst Cat nibbled on a pastry, Amy told her that a
social media influencer was due to check-in. His agent
had made the booking that morning after a newspaper
printed a front-page spread describing him as 'tired and
emotional'.

'A fourteen-day cocaine binge in Ibiza would
make me tired and emotional too,' tutted Amy then she
blushed. 'Oh! Forget I said that.'

'What's an influencer?'

'I'm not really sure.'

Cat stared up at the ceiling and sighed. The
flawless, white surface above reminded her of an ice
rink. Smooth and perfect. She liked that. She liked
white.

When she'd been a small girl, sharing a mould-
ridden room with her big sister, she had admired the
homes in the glossy magazines at the Doctors surgery.
All white walls and fresh flowers. She owned one of
those sorts of homes now.

After this break, she'd cut back her hours so that
she could enjoy her home more. She was the boss for
God's sake. It was time to let her team start taking on the
big clients. Yes, there were lots of things she would be

doing differently. A few days here had given her some perspective. How long had she been here?

'You're away with the fairies there, Catherine.' Amy interrupted her thoughts.

'Hmmm?'

'I said you're away with the fairies. What are you thinking about?'

'Oh. Nothing much.'

'Well eat up and then get yourself ready. Paul is coming to see you this morning, remember?'

'Of course I remember.' Cat did not like how the woman patronised her.

After Amy had cleared the breakfast tray and left, Cat got ready. It didn't take long, no wardrobe choices were necessary when a fluffy white gown was the dress code. Cat considered the lack of everyday decisions that needed to be made here, one of the main benefits of being on retreat.

Visitors were not allowed in the bedrooms, not even spouses, so the meeting with Paul had been arranged to take place in the vast communal lounge. There were an array of sofas, neatly arranged into groups. Paul was sitting in the furthest corner, perched on the edge of a chair, chewing his nails.

'Darling,' she went to kiss him but he shifted awkwardly and she missed.

'Sit down, Cat.'

'Thank you for the roses, my favourite.' She sat in an oversized chair opposite him.

'They were Chloe's idea.'

'I have a list for her. Can you take this down?'

'She doesn't take instructions from you anymore.' Paul closed his eyes briefly and shook his head.

Cat shrugged. 'I've had some thoughts on Coleman. We should push for thirty percent.'

'The Coleman deal is done, Cat.'

'But I-'

'We closed on it eighteen months ago. Don't you remember?' Paul asked.

Cat shook her head. 'I...I don't know.'

'But you do know why I booked you in here?'

'I was upset. You suggested I take a break. A retreat, if you will.'

'I came home last week to find you in my garden, lurking in the trees. You were trespassing again.'

'I was inspecting my fruit trees, yes. One of

them appeared to be diseased.'

'You were aggressive to Chloe when she asked you to leave,' Paul was shaking his head slowly.

'She should have been at the office. I left her a list. I have to do that, you know, she's quite dim.'

'*My* office. You aren't a partner anymore. I'm not your husband. Security escorted you from the office that morning because the restraining order prevents you from coming within fifty metres.' Paul's voice was rising and Amy, standing at a discreet distance behind Cat, stepped forward to be beside her.

'I don't understand,' Cat looked up at Amy helplessly, then back to Paul. 'It's so...confusing. I think I....'

'Cat, I bought you out when we divorced last year. You received a significant-'

'I came from nothing you know. Entirely self-made.' Cat poured herself some water from a plastic jug on the table.

'Not the story about your grandmother again.'

'She's dead now and Louise has moved to Australia.'

'I've spoken to Louise-'

'My sister can't bear for me to do better than

her. When you and I bought the Mayfair place she was green!'

'She told me that you're in rent arrears on your Grandmother's flat. What's happened to all the money, Cat?'

'I'm not good with admin. That's why I have Chloe.'

'You *don't* have Chloe.'

'She's unreliable.'

'She's with me. I mean, I'm with her. We are both worried about you.'

'Worried about how it looks,' Cat slowly sipped her water and stared at him.

'I'm sorry we hurt you, Cat but I've been fair. With the divorce, with all this! I could have you locked up.'

'I *am* locked up.'

'This is a nice place. The very best.' Paul lowered his head and continued quietly 'I will pay for whatever treatment you need, to get well here. But then I'm done, Cat. I came to tell you in person. Leave us alone.'

Catherine drained the contents of her cup. 'There are loose ends.'

'I mean it. Leave us be.' Paul's voice was firm/

'But what about the cruise?' Cat looked forlorn.

'What cruise? What are you on about?'

'I'm going to get some brochures when we go home. And a dog. What do you think about raised beds? Tulips or crocuses?''

Paul slapped his hands on his thighs and sighed loudly. 'I'm leaving.' He stood up and Cat leapt out of her seat.

'You just got here. There are birds. You like birds.'

'Please stop!' Paul shouted. He tried to move forward but Cat blocked his way.

'I think that's enough for today,' said Amy. 'I'll see Catherine back to her room. Thank you for coming, Mr Arnold.' A look passed between them. 'We'll be in touch.'

'Yes, we'll be in touch,' Cat said as Amy led her away. 'We've so much to arrange.'

On the walk back to her room, down the stark white corridors, Cat quizzed Amy about the influencer. But Amy was less forthcoming than she had been earlier and she was looking at her in a way that Cat did not like.

The shush-shush of Cat's slippered feet against

73

the tiled floor seemed loud in the silence between her and the nurse. It was like water filling her ears. She wanted Amy to say something but she could not think of anything to ask her and so she counted the doors along the corridor instead. 'Fourteen,' she said out loud when they reached her room at the end.

'Why don't you take it easy this afternoon, Catherine?' Nurse Amy said. 'Doctor Peters will be round shortly to top up your medication. Then perhaps you'd like to listen to Classical FM? I can sit with you.'

'No thank you,' Cat replied. 'I'm feeling quite tired. I had an important business meeting earlier.'

'I see. Well, I'll arrange for you to have a proper chat with Doctor Peters once he's completed his meds rounds. You can tell him all about your…meeting.'

'I'm not sure I'll be free later,' Cat said. 'I have a big client I'm working with and I can't take too much time off.'

Nurse Amy said nothing as she settled Cat back into her room. She wrote a long note, placed it inside a brown file with *Catherine Arnold* labelled on it and handed it to the Doctor when he came around to administer her medication.

Once she was alone, Cat sat in the sofa and

stared out of the locked patio doors. This really was a lovely place for a retreat. She would miss it.

She thought about Paul. The flecks of grey at his temples were flashed all through his hair now and his eyes had gained new lines in the corners. She'd been right to suggest a cruise. He looked like he needed it more than she did.

In the bedside drawer was a short pencil and her notebook which she used to scribble down thoughts, ideas and lists. This was a technique given to her by one of the therapists, to quiet the chatter in her mind. She found a blank page and wrote an affirmation. *I am smart. I find ways to get what I want.* She said the affirmation aloud a few times and yawned. Her head felt heavy.

On the cusp of sleep, Cat considered the chat she'd be having with the Doctor later. She never went to a meeting unprepared. She decided that she would agree to all his terms, it didn't do to be a hard negotiator every time. And then, when she left here, the first thing she would do would be to call the gardener about the apple tree. The second thing would be to take all of Paul's bird feeders down.

Cat curled up on the sofa. As she slipped down

the white walls onto the black floor of another blank sleep, she smiled.

THE HEART OF THE HOME

The year that Phil and I bought our house was the same year that Prince Charles and Lady Diana were married. It was a lovely little semi, in the crook of a cul-de-sac and our very first place together as newly-weds. Of course, not long after everyone was buying houses. It was the right-to-buy scheme, giving them all a headstart but we were first and we did it the proper way, on our own.

Well, almost on our own. Maureen, that's Phil's mum, chipped in a bit. In fact she was the one who had found the house, quite by accident, whilst out on one of her walks. She had hurried home and called the estate agent to book a viewing for us before she'd even told us about it. Later, it was Maureen who negotiated on price, exchange dates and so on whilst Phil encouraged her and I quietly seethed. Phil said I shouldn't play my face up so much, that his mum had more experience in these things and that she was giving us so much help with the deposit, the least we could do was involve her.

On our first viewing, the estate agent had aimed all of his patter at Maureen, who in turn had coached us like a school teacher, saying encouraging things and telling us how perfect it was. I suppose she did have an eye for potential and as we walked around, I daydreamed about how it could look once I'd put my mark on the place. There was quite a bit of work to be done but Maureen said that was to be expected for the price and that as a part of our wedding present, she would give us some help with the extra costs.

'This will make a lovely family home, Deborah,' she had said to me on the day we moved in. 'And I have it on good authority that the local school is excellent.'

'We'll soon fill the place with little ones, Mum,' Phil said proudly, putting his arm around me.

'Hmmm,' I'd replied, knowing full well that the walls would be staying free of little fingerprints for quite a while yet.

I was dead proud of the place once all the work was finished, although it took a lot longer than expected and went well over budget. I held a little Tupperware party so that all of my friends could see how the place looked with its flashy kitchen extension and mod cons. Maureen had turned up uninvited and made herself right at home, holding court in my sitting room like she owned the place. My friends lapped her up and were singing her praises for weeks afterwards.

She often called in on her walks for 'just a cuppa'. These unannounced visits would last all afternoon until Phil got in from work. I started to find excuses to be out but then Phil had a key cut for her without telling me, so she could let herself in! Imagine my shock when I came back from Kwik Save one afternoon, to find her pottering around in my kitchen, the oven on and every pan bubbling away. She didn't even say hello, just launched straight into a list of what she was cooking.

'I'll freeze it all into portions for you,' she said. 'So that Phil can have his favourites whenever he fancies them. Fatten him up a bit'

'He doesn't need fattening up.'

'Salads can't sustain a working man, dear,' and she gave me a knowing look.

'We're eating healthily, Maureen.'

She smiled then. 'Is that for, you know… baby making?'

Honestly! Her nosiness was intolerable. As soon as she was done cooking, I thanked her and packed her off to the bus stop.

Granted, her cooking *was* delicious and it was quite nice when she ironed Phil's shirts or pushed the hoover round. I just wished she would let me know when she was coming and not be here quite so much.

'She's trying to help,' Phil said, every time I brought it up. 'Plus, she's lonely.'

I suggested to him that she could find some friends her own age, seeing as though she lived in a retirement village but he went into one of his huffs. What Phil didn't appreciate was that it was me who had to occupy her, listening to her moaning about her aches and pains. Plus there had been a few embarrassing moments with her wandering in.

'We're newly-weds, Phil. It's not right that your mother is always here,' I complained. 'Put a stop to it, or I will.'

Our rows over it escalated and one night, after Phil called me ungrateful, I made him sleep in the spare room. After that, the key reappeared on its hook in the hall. Phil started calling in at Maureen's on his way home from work. She didn't seem to be going for her walks much either so I saw much less of her. I liked it that way, although I did miss her help around the house a bit.

'I don't think Mum's well,' he said after a visit one evening.

'It'll be the weather, plays havoc with old folk. Shut the door, you're letting a draft in.'

'She's only in her fifties, Deb.' He flopped down next to me and kicked off his shoes. 'Something's not right.'

'I imagine today's news has cheered her up though.'

'News?'

I pointed at the TV. 'Charles and Lady Di. They're engaged.'

'Really? They look a bit awkward together.' The camera was following the couple across a green. The Prince had his arms folded and Diana, dressed in beautiful blue, was hooked stiffly at his elbow like an umbrella.

'I was chatting to a few of the girls in the laundrette earlier,' I said. 'We're forming a Street Party Committee.'

'Street party?'

'Yes, for the wedding.'

'Right. Look, do you think you could call in on Mum tomorrow? Only, I'm doing overtime to cover the credit on that twin tub you've had and I won't finish till late.'

It was unusual of him to ask and so I agreed but I didn't get any time to pop round that week or the next.

I had my hands full with the committee and all of our planning. Plus I'd volunteered to host the television screening at our place -give me another chance to show off a bit. So, I had lots on my mind.

Now I think of it, it was probably a month until I saw Maureen. She did look a bit peaky but seemed fine in herself. She had admired the curtains I'd made for the living room and made the usual noises about the place being too big for just a couple.

I had swiftly changed the subject and filled her in on the plans that the Street Party Committee had made. She was interested, but made no mention of joining us and I wondered if Phil had warned her off. It was not like Maureen to miss a party.

The spring passed by quickly as I immersed myself in preparations with the committee. I read every article on 'how to hostess an unforgettable party', pored over the catalogues for outfit ideas and shopped for little accessories to dot around the house. The visits from Maureen dwindled to almost nothing and I was pleased that she had decided to step back a bit and let us find our own stride.

The night before the royal wedding, I could not keep still. The anticipation of having all of our neighbours round to watch the wedding had me cleaning and rearranging everything. As I put the last bottle into the drinks cabinet and ran my duster over it's shiny top I smiled with satisfaction.

'I'm so excited for tomorrow, aren't you?' I asked Phil.

'I'm glad for the day off. I'm knackered.'

'There are people camping out on the mall. I saw it on the news earlier.'

He pulled a face. 'Over two million unemployed and Thatcher can find money for a bloody wedding.'

'Don't be a spoil sport. I've done cheese and pineapple hedgehogs, you love those.'

'I'll have something out of there, get me in the mood,' he said, reaching for the cabinet.

'You will not! They're for tomorrow.'

Phil shook his head and turned his attention back to Bergerac. The phone rang then but I didn't get up. As sure as night follows day, it would be Maureen, checking in.

Phil grabbed it and before he could finish reciting our number I saw his face fall. 'I'm on my way,' he said.

'What's the matter?'

'That was Mum's neighbour, Alan. He had to call an ambulance for her. I've got to go.' He snatched his car keys from the telephone table and rushed out before I could respond.

He was still not back when I went to bed. I tried to wait up but I was worn out from the day I'd had and when I came downstairs the next morning, I found him asleep in the armchair. A gap in the curtains, from where I'd mismeasured, had painted a streak of sunlight across his face which was scrunched up like a wrung out flannel. He murmured when I pulled the curtains back.

I was impressed when I looked out. Brightly coloured hanging baskets adorned every house, bunting looped from tree to tree and Charles and Di posters were up in several of the windows. Beyond our cul-de-sac, red, white and blue pennants could be seen from the nearby pub and community centre.

Despite the early hour, two men were unloading trestle tables a few doors down. I opened the window and the faint sound of Bucks Fizz drifted from their van.

'What time is it? Phil sat up. He was still wearing his clothes from the night before.

'Just after seven. I'll make you a coffee and you can fill me in.'

'I've got to get back to the hospital.'

'It looks like you've only just got in, you're knackered.' But he was already heading upstairs. 'Phil!' I called. 'I promised the committee that you'd set the barbecue up.' The bathroom door slammed and he was gone soon after without saying goodbye.

Around ten thirty, our neighbours began arriving. I dashed back and forth, topping up sherries, opening the door to more guests and keeping an eye on both the BBC and my oven. Not for the first time, it occurred to me that I could have done with Maureen's help. She was a real pro at parties, never frazzled.

Within an hour almost the whole street was huddled around my television. Every flat surface had someone perched on it and the drinks cabinet was devoid of it's neatly arranged bottles. Then the bride appeared at the steps of St. Paul's Cathedral and there was a momentary hush in the room before everyone started talking at once, cooing over the ivory silk taffeta.

I didn't hear Phil return. He just appeared in the doorway, looking crumpled and confused. His eyes were red and darting back and forth, like an abacus, counting all of our visitors.

'Phil?' I said, taking in his sagging shoulders.

'She's gone.'

'What?' I glanced back at the TV. The bride's train had to be at least twenty foot. It stretched out behind her like an ocean, rippling as she walked.

'Mum. She's gone.'

'Gone where?' Maybe twenty-five foot. I'd never seen anything like it.

'She died just after eight. It was her heart. Doc said she's been having trouble for ages.'

'Oh Phil! How awful,' I cried. Like an audience seeing the conductor's baton raise, the neighbours around us fell silent.

'It explains all this,' he threw his arms wide. 'This house. The money. She knew she didn't have long.' Someone got up and switched off the television, just as the camera caught Prince Charles turning.

'Let's go into the kitchen,' I said firmly. 'Everyone, do help yourselves to a Cinzano. If there's any left that is.' I didn't need eyes in the back of my head to see the awkward looks being exchanged behind me.

Phil went to the kitchen and slumped into a seat at the breakfast bar, unspeaking and unblinking. I sat beside him and held his hand. It trembled.

In the next room, I could hear movement as our neighbours began leaving, talking in low voices. They made their way out quickly and round to the house next-door.

When the last person had left, Phil spoke. 'Do you know what she said to one of the nurses at her last appointment?' Before I could reply he continued. 'That she could go now, that she knew we were set up for a family life. That she'd done her bit.'

'Yes, she'd done her bit.' I echoed. Phil fell silent again but tightened his grip on my hand. I couldn't think of anything else to say.

Through the adjoining wall, I could hear the neighbours congregating, their tones animated again. A cheer went up, pulling Phil from his daze.

'They're celebrating,' I explained.

'Oh,' he said and then burst into tears.

I held him, awkwardly at first, stooped over him as he sat and sobbed into his hands. Then he stood and we embraced fully for a long time. It occurred to me that we had not held one another like that since our wedding day but I didn't know why not.

I looked around the kitchen. *The heart of the home* I had called it proudly when the builders had finished but

Maureen had opined that it was family that made a home, not the bricks and mortar. Phil and I stayed there all afternoon, talking, crying, remembering. We didn't join in with street celebrations and I didn't mind. It was just the two of us now.

DAD'S WIFE

She strutted down the church aisle, her heels tapping out a staccato. I shuffled behind, choking down the fog of her perfume. Dad was slightly ahead of us.

Her blonde bob swayed across the shoulders of her red coat. I wished I had done something with my own hair, which was mousey brown like Dad's.

The gatherers in black nodded solemnly in our direction as we took our seats in the front pew. She placed her leather tote between us, a designer barricade paid for with Dad's money.

Dad was in front of the altar now, cased in elaborately decorated oak.

SUSIE'S ROOM

I tucked my sleeping daughter into bed and kissed her lightly on her smooth forehead.

As I looked up, I caught a glimpse of Susie. She stood silently in the corner watching. The night light cast an eerie glow across her overly made-up face. She stared at me, her eyes unblinking pools of bright blue. I looked away quickly.

I moved quietly around the room, picking up discarded clothes and toys. A plastic block slipped from my clammy palm onto the floor, the light clatter making me jump. I could feel Susie's glare on my back.

Silently chastising myself, I grabbed her by her spongy head and tossed her into the toybox.

ABOUT THE AUTHOR

Michelle Mclean was born and resides in the West Midlands. Stories have always been a part of her life and she knew from an early age that she wanted to write them.

Reading is an important part of Michelle's writing practice and she can always be found with a notebook and a novel. After regularly hearing others say how little time they had to read, the idea for *Teabreak Tales* was born.

Michelle's writing 'routine' is to snatch time to write whenever it presents itself and this is often whilst commuting. Eavesdropping and observing whilst travelling to work provided rich writing prompts, some of the results of which have made their way into this book.

Michelle is currently a student at the University of Birmingham studying MA Creative Writing. This is her first published collection of short stories, though many more are hiding in her notebooks.